'TWAS HALLOWEEN EVENING

A Tale of the Zombie Apocalypse

Cheralyn Lambeth

PROSPECTIVE PRESS

Winston-Salem

P R O S P E C T I V E   P R E S S LLC

1959 Peace Haven Rd, #246, Winston-Salem, NC 27106 U.S.A.
www.prospectivepress.com

Published in the United States of America by PROSPECTIVE PRESS LLC

'TWAS HALLOWEEN EVENING
A TALE OF THE ZOMBIE APOCALYPSE

ISBN 978-1-943419-94-4

First PROSPECTIVE PRESS softcover edition

Printed in the United States of America
First printing November 2019

The text of this book is typeset in Minion Pro and Creepshow

PUBLISHER'S NOTE

Introduction and Acknowledgments

A few years ago, I belonged to an informal writers' group that would meet on weekends to discuss our various writing projects. Occasionally we'd be given an assignment to complete and bring in for our next meeting, and one such assignment was to write a drabble on the Zombie Apocalypse (a drabble being a short fictional story about 100 words in length; the idea is to see how well you can tell an interesting story in a short amount of space). I dutifully set out to compose my drabble, and found as I went that it seemed to take on a life of its own; the end result being this parody of 'Twas the Night Before Christmas (with sincere apologies to Clement Moore).

The response from my writers' group and other readers was encouraging, so much so that I toyed with the idea of self-publishing it as a parody coffee table book, and even pitched the idea to several publishers. It was a chance encounter with Jason Graves of Prospective Press publishing at ConGregate convention in 2018 that led to the book being accepted for publication, and I'm extremely grateful to Jason and the other staff at Prospective Press for believing in my project.

I also owe thanks to my fellow writers in the Emerald Isle writers' group for their advice and support: Janine Spendlove, Ronald Garner, Cricket Bauer, Amber Biles, Rich Sigfrit, Ivana Spendlove, and in particular, Aaron Allston.

Lastly, I owe a great deal of thanks to my fellow "zombie hunters" Chuck Carte and Marc Fleming for their assistance in creating the illustrations used in this book: to Chuck for building several of the tombstones used as set dressing, and to both Chuck and Marc for patiently posing for the dozens of photos used as reference.

Thank you all—I couldn't have done this without you!

Dedicated to the memory of

Aaron Allston,

And to

George A. Romero

Who started it all.

'Twas Halloween evening, and all through the night,

We humans were hunting for zombies to fight.

The weapons were gathered and loaded with care,

Ready to blast any zombies out there.

And I in my armor, with rifle in hand,
Was just scoping out the lay of the land,

When in the graveyard there arose such a clatter,
I reached for my gun — I knew what was the matter.

The moon glinting off of the tombstones below

Gave the entire graveyard an unearthly glow,

When what to my wondering eyes should appear
But a sight to cause even the bravest to fear.

An army of zombies appeared with a cry,
And I knew at that moment we must fight — or die.

More rapid than eagles the zombies they ran,
And I suddenly realized we'd need a new plan,

For we were outnumbered a hundred to one,
And the only thing we could do now was to run.

"To the old iron gate! Past the cemetery wall!
Now run away! Run away! RUN AWAY ALL!"

As leaves in the wind from the zombies we flew,
In a desperate attempt to escape from the grue,

Past headstone and footstone we flew through the yard,

Out through the main gate, we slammed shut, good and hard.

But then, in a twinkling, I heard at the gate,
The sound of the lock being ripped from the grate,

As I drew in a breath and was turning around,
The whole horde of zombies leapt out with a bound.

They were dressed all in rags from their heads to their toes,
And ashes and dirt covered all of their clothes,

Their gray skin was mottled and tarnished with mold,
And they looked such a horrible sight to behold.

Their eyes — how they glowered! Their faces — how scary!
Each nose sunk and black like a half-rotted cherry,

Their lips were drawn back in an unearthly howl,
And each one emitted an odor most foul.

The stump of an arm one held clenched in his teeth,

And one carried with him his funeral wreath.

But... something seemed not quite right, as they drew near,
And I laughed, when I saw them, in spite of my fear,

For the wink of an eye, and the nod of a head,
Soon gave me to know we had nothing to dread.

They spoke not a word, but just then we could tell,
That these were not true zombies under a spell,

But just Halloween revelers out for some fun
And, now we'd been frightened, their work here was done.

They turned to go slowly, as if moving through tar,
And away they all staggered like drunks from a bar,

But I heard one exclaim, as they lurched out of sight,
"Happy Halloween, all, and to all, a good fright!"

About the Author

Cheralyn Lambeth is a professional costume, prop, and puppet builder whose work includes feature films (The Muppet Christmas Carol, The Patriot, Evan Almighty, The Hunger Games), television programs (Dinosaurs!, Homeland, Outcast), and live/interactive properties (Avenue Q, Star Trek: The Experience, Sir Purr for the Carolina Panthers). She is excited to be publishing her first fiction book with Prospective Press, adding it to her list of non-fiction publications (*Haunted Theaters of the Carolinas*, *Creating the Character Costume*, and *Introduction to Puppetry Arts*).